Samuel French Acting Edition

I0591849

Leveling Up
(Virtually)

by Deborah Zoe Laufer

ıl SAMUEL FRENCH lı

MUSIC AND THIRD-PARTY MATERIALS USE NOTE

IMPORTANT BILLING AND CREDIT REQUIREMENTS

LEVELING UP (VIRTUALLY) was adapted from the stage version by Deborah Zoe Laufer.

Development of the stage version was supported by the Eugene O'Neill Theater Center during a residency at the National Playwrights Conference, 2011 (Preston Whiteway, Executive Director, Wendy C. Goldberg, Artistic Director). It premiered at Cincinnati Playhouse in the Park at the Thompson Shelterhouse in Cincinnati, Ohio on February 9, 2013, directed by Wendy C. Goldberg.

CHARACTERS

IAN – (Early 20s) Awesome gamer – Nevada State champ. Very bright. Finds it hard to interact off-screen. Loves Jeannie and hates himself for it.

CHUCK – (Early 20s) All around good guy. The peacemaker, Chuck wants everyone to be happy. To get along. Loves Jeannie.

ZANDER – (Early 20s) Very good looking. A wheeler dealer, but lost.

JEANNIE – (21) Zan's girlfriend. Serious psych. student, in her last year of college. Sweet and optimistic, Jeannie soaks up everything she learns.

SETTING

Online. Las Vegas.

TIME

2012.

AUTHOR'S NOTES

LEVELING UP is played in ten scenes without an intermission.

Occasionally, we see the games that they are playing, (it can establish the following scene), but usually we just see them playing, and hear the game's unique sounds.

A slash (/) in a line indicates overlap – where there is a slash, the next character begins speaking. If overlap is problematic on your online platform, simply cut the words after the slash.

(Four video conferencing boxes. In each we can see four different games* being played: a war game, a fantasy game, a racing game, a life-simulation game. They are being played by each of the four characters.)

(Alone in their rooms. Alone in their games.)

(Alone.)

(The cacophony increases and then Zap. The games bump out.)

---

* A license to produce *Leveling Up (Virtually)* does not include a license to publicly display any third-party or copyrighted images. Licensees must acquire rights for any copyrighted images or create their own. For further information, please see the Music and Third Party Materials Use Note on page iii.

Scene One

(The whole screen is taken up with a Call of Duty-*type* war game. We watch for a moment.)*

(Then the game disappears and we see **JEANNIE** *and* **CHUCK**, *in their own small apartments, deeply engaged in a military operation.* **CHUCK** *is delighted to be teaching the most awesome girl ever (even if she is Zan's girlfriend). Their speech is high energy – they sometimes strain to be heard over the game.)*

JEANNIE. Because... I should live first.

CHUCK. Right?

JEANNIE. Get some real-life experience. With actual kids.

CHUCK. Totally.

JEANNIE. But of course, my parents are like – *what*? I mean, everyone in my family went to med school – my siblings and / my...

CHUCK. Cool. Move around to the other side of the roof. I'm gonna shoot that guy. Please head shot, please head shot. YES!

JEANNIE. Ewwww. That was...

CHUCK. Awesome, right?!

JEANNIE. *(Laughing.)* OK...

CHUCK. Try to stay behind me.

JEANNIE. K.

---

* A license to produce *Leveling Up (Virtually)* does not include a license to publicly display any third-party or copyrighted images. Licensees must acquire rights for any copyrighted images or create their own. For further information, please see the Music and Third Party Materials Use Note on page iii.

So, I'm taking the MCATS in case I want to be a psychiatrist eventually, but really, I'm like – why? To dole out pills? When what I really want is to interact with actual kids you / know?

CHUCK. Totally.

JEANNIE. In troubled neighborhoods. See what it's like in the trenches.

CHUCK. Right. Watch out here, we're surrounded.

JEANNIE. Not that there aren't plenty of troubled kids in regular schools, but if I go to some troubled neighborhoods, I think could really make a difference.

CHUCK. Ya, troubled neighborhoods – totally where you find the troubled kids.

JEANNIE. I mean, when you were in middle school, would you / have...

CHUCK. Let's go to that other rooftop.

JEANNIE. Oh. How do I...

CHUCK. You make him jump with the spacebar. See?

JEANNIE. Oh!

Would you have ever gone to your school psychologist with a real problem?

CHUCK. Nah.

JEANNIE. No way, right? And I so want to be that person, you know? Who the kids / feel...

CHUCK. Sure. Space bar. To jump.

JEANNIE. ...they can come to.

CHUCK. When they're troubled. Right.

JEANNIE. Does that sounds stupid? Like who the hell am I / that

CHUCK. Not at all! Jump! Spacebar! Spacebar!!

(She pushes it just in time.)

JEANNIE. Oh! Thanks.

CHUCK. Sure. No. It's totally awesome that you care. I mean so few people really...

JEANNIE. I do. I love kids. I really want to help.

(She shoots one of their own.)

CHUCK. Ahhh!

JEANNIE. Oh no! Sorry.

CHUCK. *(Trying not to be upset.)* No. It's cool.

JEANNIE. I just shot one of our own.

CHUCK. Happens all the time dude. Friendly fire. You're gonna lose some points though.

JEANNIE. *(She laughs.)* I can't believe I'm even playing this!

CHUCK. You're doing great.

JEANNIE. Thanks. Did you apply to grad school? When you / finished...

CHUCK. Nah. Stay behind debris and stuff, OK? Did you see that sniper? You almost got shot.

JEANNIE. Oops. Sorry.

CHUCK. No. You're doing great.

JEANNIE. Thanks for killing him.

CHUCK. Call of duty baby.

JEANNIE. Hah!

CHUCK. I got your back.

(IAN pops on the screen, extremely agitated.)

IAN. Where's Zander?

JEANNIE. Hi Ian.

IAN. I went to his place, he's not there.

CHUCK. E-man! You were out in the real world?

IAN. Have you seen him?

Jeannie?!

JEANNIE. He was supposed to be on here, like...

IAN. *(Texting* **ZAN.***)* I've been texting him for an hour!

(**IAN** *walks off screen.*)

CHUCK & JEANNIE. *(A crash.)* Nooooo!!!

CHUCK. *(Calling to* **IAN.***)* Hey. Didjahear from that guy again, E?

JEANNIE. Oh no! Chuck!

CHUCK. Ouch. Sorry dude.

JEANNIE. You hit me!

CHUCK. Shit. We need to find a tank and get out of here.

JEANNIE. But I'm...dead now.

CHUCK. You're fine. See?

JEANNIE. What?

CHUCK. Pick yourself up. Dust yourself off...

JEANNIE. *(Laughing.)* Oh. Cool!

IAN. *(Reentering.)* Where is he??

CHUCK. Follow me.

IAN. Jeannie?

JEANNIE. He was supposed to be on here, like... Yikes! Like hours ago. Why?

CHUCK. Nice save.

JEANNIE. Thanks.

CHUCK. *(To* IAN.) Dude, you hear from that suit again?

IAN. *(His phone.)* God, Zan! Pick up!

JEANNIE. What suit?

CHUCK. This creepy army dude is stalking Ian.

JEANNIE. Army dude?

IAN. *(Very important – to impress* JEANNIE.*)* The NSA.

JEANNIE. Wait. What?

CHUCK. Yeah, they called me, asking all these questions about him. They called his parents. His old professors. Uncle Sam wants you dude.

JEANNIE. For a job? The army?

IAN. The NSA. National Security Agency.

JEANNIE. Wow. What job?

IAN. If I tell you I'll have to kill you.

CHUCK. Are you gonna go? For the interview?

IAN. Nah.

CHUCK. Fuck, you should go dude.

IAN. Holy shit. Is that *Final Kill III*?

CHUCK. Oh yeah, baby.

IAN. That's not out till next week!

CHUCK. Maybe for you.

IAN. How'd you get that? They broke the street date?

CHUCK. I have my ways.

IAN. Stellar graphics.

CHUCK. Right?

(Some catastrophe.)

IAN. Ooooo. Epic fail. You guys suck.

JEANNIE. *(Laughing.)* We do. We really / do.

CHUCK. Well, Jeannie sucks.

JEANNIE. Shut up! Why you need Zander?

CHUCK. Noooob *(Like rube.)*. Bringing me down to your level.

IAN. He fucking sold my Exponent Potency Mask of the Algorith.

CHUCK. What?

IAN. On eBay.

CHUCK. Holy shit.

JEANNIE. Your... Exponent...?

IAN. He auctioned it off.

JEANNIE. What's an / Ex...?

CHUCK. Exponent Potency Mask of the Algorith. It's this friggin' awesome, virtual... How much he get for it?

IAN. Last time I give that asshole my code.

JEANNIE. Z wouldn't do that – sell your...

IAN. I have the check. He fucking left a check in my mailbox. He kept ten percent, and wrote me a check for the rest.

CHUCK. How much?

IAN. It's shit, man.

CHUCK. How much shit?

IAN. Nine. *(Kicking a chair.)* Dammit!

CHUCK. He got ten k for that thing?

JEANNIE. Wait. Ten thousand...dollars?

CHUCK. Dude. That's awesome.

JEANNIE. Ten thousand real American dollars?

CHUCK. I mean, isn't that awesome?

JEANNIE. For a make-believe mask?

IAN. *(Deeply insulted.) Make believe??* That was a level thirty Exponent Potency Mask of the Algorith. That mask – you put on that mask and you could do anything. Be anyone. Plus 53 Stamina. Plus 42 Agility. Increases your critical strike by ninety-fucking-seven.

You know how many quests I won to level it up that high? You put on that mask, you enter the Jinpo Pakosphere, and you can defeat anyone.

(ZANDER joins them online.)

ZANDER. All hail the conquering hero!

IAN. Asshole!

ZANDER. Whoa. Ian. Did you see what I got you?

IAN. I saw what you left me.

ZANDER. Well, yeah, I took a percentage.

IAN. Stole.

ZANDER. Dude. It's a broker's fee. Most of it's going to you anyway, for what I owe you.

JEANNIE. Hey babe.

ZANDER. Hey babe. Chuckstein *(Like Einstein.)*.

CHUCK. Hey.

IAN. You owe me twenty thousand dollars, Zander.

ZANDER. What?

CHUCK. Whoa.

IAN. That was a year's work there. That fucking mask is worth thirty k.

CHUCK. Holy shit.

JEANNIE. Wait. / What?

ZANDER. No Ian no. I asked around. I mean, I didn't sell to the first guy. I got offered five k at first. I bargained it up. You should have seen me. / I...

IAN. I could have sold that mask for thirty thousand dollars. I would have lived off it for like, FOREVER! And now, how the hell am I gonna see that money? *You're* never gonna get it! God!

> (**IAN** *kicks a chair. He stalks about his apartment, coming back on screen to rage at* **ZANDER.**)

CHUCK. Dude. Chill.

ZANDER. That mask was worth thirty? No way.

IAN. A guy in China just got thirty k for a mask that didn't have half the powers of my mask.

ZANDER. Wow E, I'm totally sorry. You should have said something. I mean, I had no idea it was worth thirty. / Wow.

IAN. What should I have said? "Oh, by the way, please don't go sneaking into my account which I entrusted the code to you, and steal my mask?" Gee. It never occurred to me to tell you that.

ZANDER. You were going to get thirty for that mask? That's insane dude. That's totally...

IAN. What's insane is that you sold it for nothing. Dammit.

> (*He kicks the chair.*)

CHUCK. Easy on the chair E.

JEANNIE. (*To* **ZANDER.**) Call the guy back. The guy you sold it to. Tell him it was a mistake.

ZANDER. Babe.

JEANNIE. If you explain to him that it wasn't really your mask...maybe he'll understand.

IAN. And he'll just offer to pay an extra twenty grand.

JEANNIE. It's worth a try.

IAN. What planet do you live on?

CHUCK. Ian.

ZANDER. I'm so sorry dude. Wow. Here, I thought I was gonna like...surprise you that I got this crazy dude to pay...

IAN. Yeah. I'm surprised.

JEANNIE. Well, it's in a game, right? Can't you just make another one?

IAN. Make another one.

JEANNIE. I mean, you did it once, right?

IAN. Do you know what it takes to get to that level? Only one other person in the WORLD has gotten to that level. And it was the guy in China. And he sold it for thirty k. By the time I get there again, everybody will have gotten there and it's going to be worth shit. You're all so...ignorant.

ZANDER. Hey. Come on.

IAN. You are. You're...

> *(It's pointless. Kicks the chair and hurts himself.)*

Ow. Whatever. Forget it.

> *(He sits and starts playing his own war game.)*

CHUCK. He'll get you the money.

IAN. Right.

CHUCK. *(To* **ZANDER.***)* Dude. You have to get him that money.

IAN. Forget it, Chuck.

JEANNIE. No. He will. Right hon?

ZANDER. Yeah, wow. I mean, I had no idea it was worth that much. Are you / sure...

JEANNIE. But you have to. Pay him back.

IAN. Jeannie. He doesn't *do* anything. Don't you get that?

ZANDER. What's that supposed to mean?

JEANNIE. He does things.

IAN. Ummm...no.

JEANNIE. He'll get a job. He'll pay you back a little at a time.

IAN. Uh huh.

JEANNIE. Right babe?

CHUCK. Ou...ch. *(A bomb exploding at the end.)*

ZANDER. Right.

IAN. What job? Ahhh! Forget it.

JEANNIE. He's had jobs. Right Z?

CHUCK. Yeah, the thing is, with a job, you kind of have to show up.

IAN. He gets money off his parents. Don't you know that? All while I was working to pay for school...

ZANDER. Working?

IAN. His parents just sent him money.

ZANDER. Not any more!

IAN. Yeah, I noticed.

JEANNIE. Why don't you sell things too? Masks and swords or whatnot. There must be other things worth a lot, I mean, you play tons.

CHUCK. Jeannie. Dude. Zan is totally not at that level.

ZANDER. Hey. I'm plenty respectable.

CHUCK. I mean, nothing personal dude, but that shit that Ian does, what he's capable of...that's like...it's like not even human. It's like not even in the same universe.

ZANDER. I've leveled up. Plenty. I was on level 37 on Quasar B. I had three level 70s with six more alts in the 30-45 range. But you know, I play a variety of games and Ian / just...

CHUCK. No way. Ian is like an artist. He's a total Nevcom genius.

JEANNIE. Yeah?

CHUCK. He was Nevada champion two years in a row. You didn't know that?

JEANNIE. Wow.

CHUCK. Nevada State Champion. *(To* ZANDER.) You didn't tell her that dude?

ZANDER. Yeah / I did.

JEANNIE. Wow. No.

CHUCK. You are like, in the presence of greatness here.

IAN. *(Flattered.)* Shut up.

CHUCK. I'm serious dude. We are not worthy.

ZANDER. Well, excuse me if I'm not at his level, but, you know, I have a life. I don't play twenty hours a day.

CHUCK. You kinda do man.

ZANDER. I have a real life in the real world.

IAN. What? What is your real life?

ZANDER. I have a girlfriend.

IAN. What does that mean? You're good at...what?

CHUCK. Getting a girlfriend!

JEANNIE. Ummm... I'm right here, so...

ZANDER. That's more than you dude. I mean, where's your girlfriend?

JEANNIE. Guys.

ZANDER. Have you *ever* had a girlfriend?

CHUCK. Zan.

IAN. You're saying you're superior to me because you have a girlfriend.

ZANDER. No. I'm saying I have a LIFE because I have a girlfriend.

IAN. *(Stymied.)* What the fuck. I have been fucking CARRYING you on my back since college.

ZANDER. That's bullshit.

IAN. Who paid your last three months' rent?

ZANDER. I just left you a check for it!

IAN. YOU LEFT ME A CHECK OFF THE MONEY YOU STOLE FROM ME!

CHUCK. Owned!

IAN. You owe me all that rent and twenty thousand dollars.

ZANDER. That's your real life. You're a loan shark.

IAN. Are you fucking out of your mind? I was doing you a / favor!

JEANNIE. Guys. Stop. Come on. You're best friends. Stop it.

ZANDER. Ian dude. I'm sorry about the mask. That was totally fucked of me and I'm sorry. I'll get you that money. I will. Somehow, I'll get it.

JEANNIE. Of course you will. Of course you'll pay him back. You're friends. That's what's really important.

CHUCK. Totally.

JEANNIE. This was a terrible mistake, but Zander will make it up to you.

You guys should just like, go out for a beer or something, you know? Or a movie? Get outside and hang out, right?

CHUCK. Outside?

IAN. I'm meeting a bunch of guys on Paraquad. But thanks.

JEANNIE. Online?

CHUCK. Cool! Can you share screen?

IAN. Sure.

> (**IAN** *fires up his game.* **CHUCK** *and* **ZAN** *are mesmerized watching him play.*)

JEANNIE. Let's get out in the fresh air. Go for a walk or something. We'll all feel better.

> (*They don't even hear her.*)

I was reading in my Psych 3 about internet addiction, which I'm *not* saying you have – at *all*, I'm just saying they think it's associated with reduced levels of dopaminergic receptor availability in the striatum.

> (*All three flinch at something that happens in* **IAN***'s game.*)

Which basically means, it can make you like totally depressed.

CHUCK. Huh. That's really interesting.

JEANNIE. Dopamine is a powerful drug.

ZANDER. That's fascinating babe. Maybe you're depressed E-man.

IAN. *(Playing intently.)* I'm depressed you fucking gave away my fucking mask for fucking nothing!

ZANDER. Yeah, but listen – Jeannie's right. You do take this whole gaming thing too seriously.

IAN. What??

ZANDER. You need more dopamine. You need to get off the screen. For your own good. You need to get a life man.

IAN. I have – ALL OF THIS. *(Pointing to all his equipment.)* I bought all of this, AND all your shit. With gaming money, with tournament money, with money I EARN! Leveling up other people, selling swords, magna clubs...

ZANDER. Out of this box, I mean. You have nothing out of / this...

IAN. And you play it as much as I do. You play all day and all night and you don't sleep and you forget to go to work and you stand up your girlfriend and all your "real life" things that are so fantastic, because you play as much as I do. More. But you are BAD at it. If I put in as many hours as you do at something, and I was still bad at it, I'd freaking kill myself.

(There is a silence. Everyone is shocked by the force of that statement.)

ZANDER. Wow.

JEANNIE. He's just upset honey. We should / all...

ZANDER. No. I'm done. That's fine. I'm done. I'm not playing any more.

CHUCK. Dude. Don't even say that.

IAN. Good. Go get some dopamine.

ZANDER. And I'm not taking any more rent money from you. That's it. I'll live on the street if I have to.

CHUCK. Yo. Guys. This is all totally extreme.

ZANDER. *(To* **JEANNIE.***)* Or... Hey, babe! Maybe I'll move in with you! Wouldn't that be awesome? If we...

JEANNIE. Well...my roommates would kind of freak / if...

CHUCK. Guys. Come on. Let's just chill. Want to meet up on the quad? Maybe grab a burger?

JEANNIE. That's a great idea!

CHUCK. My treat!

> *(Pause.)*

Guys?

ZANDER. Look. E. I'll find a way to pay you back.

IAN. Yeah.

ZANDER. No. I will. I'm sorry. I didn't think... I didn't know it was worth that much.

IAN. It was the whole breaking into my system and...

ZANDER. No, I know. That was fucked up. I'm sorry.

IAN. OK.

ZANDER. Yeah? We're cool?

> *(Pause.)*

IAN. I have a life.

ZANDER. OK.

IAN. I do. I have...people...in my life. *(Referring to the screen.)* I'm playing with them right now.

ZANDER. Well...

IAN. What?

ZANDER. They're not real. This is what we're saying.

IAN. They're not real people. On their systems. Just like I am. Those are not real people.

ZANDER. The gamers are real but you don't actually know them. In the world. I mean, dude, you don't actually ever leave your room.

IAN. I do so.

ZANDER. Well...not really. I mean, barely.

(There is a beat as they all process that.)

IAN. *(Referring to outside.)* What makes that so much better?

CHUCK. Reality dude.

IAN. No really, why should I do that instead of this?

JEANNIE. Ian, you can't spend your whole life playing games.

IAN. I am making a living. A real living. Most people spend fifty hours a week at some job they freakin' hate and go home to people they find boring and it's the same fucking thing day after day...

JEANNIE. But it doesn't have to be like that. Real life can have meaning, Ian. Striving for some goal, that will bring, you know...satisfaction, and, and joy, and...

IAN. Where's the epic win in life?

There's no epic win. Ever.

JEANNIE. Epic win?

IAN. Where's the noble quest that requires a band of really smart, capable people.

CHUCK. Or Klarnogs, or Santorgs.

IAN. Those people I work with – those people – I can choose who I am, who I want to be – I can be myself with those people.

CHUCK. Or a Klarnog. Or a Santorg.

IAN. They don't care what I look like. They don't want to make idiotic small talk about things I don't care about or know about – all that superficial crap. It's not about that there. They show up and they work at optimum capacity so we can all achieve our goals. Fucking awesome talented, smart – those are my people. That's who I spend my time with.

You may think it's less real because we've never been in the same room, but that just shows your limitations, not mine. Those people I play with – none of them would ever use my code and break in and...

ZANDER. Fuck! I said I was sorry!! And you don't know that. You don't know a fucking thing about those people.

IAN. I know them better than I know you.

JEANNIE. Wow.

CHUCK. E.

(*Pause.*)

JEANNIE. Ian, finding someone to love is like that epic win, you know? Thrilling, surprising things can happen. Really. Any day something amazing might happen if you just go out and look for it. That day Zan asked me out...

ZAN. Aww babe.

(**CHUCK** *makes a gagging noise.*)

JEANNIE. You need to go out and find someone who makes you feel like life is worth living.

(*Pause.* **IAN** *is struck hard by this.*)

ZANDER. Dude. Ian. I'm sorry, man. I am.

IAN. Uh huh.

ZANDER. And I will. Pay you back. Get a...job. I will. A real job.

IAN. Ya. Me too.

CHUCK. What?

IAN. I'm gonna get a real job. In the real world. Faster than you.

ZANDER. You are?

IAN. Yeah. I'm going to fucking get that job with the NSA.

Scene Two

(JEANNIE and CHUCK have begun a Sims-like*
game. He is creating her character.)

JEANNIE. Isn't it depressing?

CHUCK. You've never been?

JEANNIE. Nah.

CHUCK. You live in Vegas and you've never gone? Dude.

JEANNIE. I just turned twenty-one.

CHUCK. Happy Birthday! You're a grown-up!

JEANNIE. *(Laughing.)* Like you're a grown-up.

CHUCK. You've got to come in some time. I'll show you around.

JEANNIE. Don't you see awful things? People losing everything...

CHUCK. It's pretty intense.

There.

JEANNIE. That haircut is so cute! I love it.

CHUCK. Good. Now we have to dress you.

JEANNIE. I'm dressed.

CHUCK. That's standard issue. We'll find something that's more "you."

JEANNIE. Oh! Fun!

So why did you choose black jack? Or do they choose for / you?

---

* A license to produce *Leveling Up (Virtually)* does not include a license to publicly display any third-party or copyrighted images. Licensees must acquire rights for any copyrighted images or create their own. For further information, please see the Music and Third Party Materials Use Note on page iii.

CHUCK. I used to deal Roulette, but I hated it. It's all luck. And these guys think they've got a strategy. I'm like, dude – wake up. There is no strategy.

Here, I'll give you some credits.

JEANNIE. Can't I earn them?

CHUCK. Oh, you'll pay me back. Mwah hah hah.

JEANNIE. *(Laughing.)* Yikes.

CHUCK. OK. You have 200.

JEANNIE. Wow, that's a lot. Are you sure...

CHUCK. You don't even know what they are!

Here. Let me take you to the store.

JEANNIE. So, isn't black jack just luck?

CHUCK. Yeah, but there's skill too. And these guys, card counters, they try to beat the system, and sometimes they do. It's a real game, you know? If you can't win, it's not a real game.

JEANNIE. But working all night. Don't you lose track of...

CHUCK. Totally. No windows. No clocks. Weird lights. It's the twilight zone.

JEANNIE. Like these little boxes!

CHUCK. Hah, right?

JEANNIE. OK. So now what do I do?

CHUCK. Let's shop. Stop me when you see a top you like.

JEANNIE. Is there something else you want to do? Like a career or...

CHUCK. Nope. Stop me when you see one.

JEANNIE. No. No. Eww. Stop! That's cute!

CHUCK. What??

JEANNIE. Why not?

CHUCK. Too frumpy.

JEANNIE. It's a peasant blouse.

CHUCK. Let's keep looking.

JEANNIE. Fine. No. No.

CHUCK. Ahhh! Yes!

JEANNIE. Chuck!

CHUCK. What??

JEANNIE. I would never wear that!

CHUCK. Jeannie. This is a chance to expand your comfort zone. Risk free. What color do you like?

JEANNIE. Blue.

CHUCK. Which blue. Here, let me...

JEANNIE. That one!

CHUCK. Peacock. Nice. You're gonna look hot in that.

JEANNIE. Maybe my character isn't hot.

CHUCK. I have a feeling she's way hot. Skirt or jeans. Or shorts?

JEANNIE. What do you like?

CHUCK. Up to you.

JEANNIE. Oh, now it's up to me?

CHUCK. It's always up to you. I'm just the facilitator.

JEANNIE. Skirt.

CHUCK. Excellent choice.

JEANNIE. That's cute.

CHUCK. Jeannie. My grandmother has a skirt like that.

JEANNIE. This is what... Daphne likes.

CHUCK. Daphne. Nice.

JEANNIE. Who are you?

CHUCK. I'm Earl.

JEANNIE. Earl.

CHUCK. I think Daphne would wear...this skirt.

JEANNIE. Daphne would not leave the house in that skirt.

CHUCK. Maybe she's staying in today.

JEANNIE. Chuck.

CHUCK. How about these shoes?

JEANNIE. Oh my God. How about you get Earl those shoes?

CHUCK. Earl would look fantastic in those shoes. Boom! Mine.

JEANNIE. Really?

CHUCK. Expanding my comfort zone. Risk free. Here's a cute little handbag. You look awesome.

JEANNIE. Don't let Daphne's mom see her in that outfit.

CHUCK. Daphne's mom lives like four hundred miles away. In... Fresno.

JEANNIE. Daphne did not grow up in Fresno!

CHUCK. Daphne is new in town. And Earl is gonna show her around. Here. I'm giving you the controls.

(He types something in.)

JEANNIE. You keep Daphne. I want to make up my own person.

CHUCK. Look, later you can pick out some more things for Earl. Though, he has kind of an extensive wardrobe already.

(**JEANNIE** *laughs.*)

Come to Earl's pad, Daphne.

JEANNIE. I don't think I should.

CHUCK. You definitely should.

JEANNIE. Well, just a few minutes. I need to study before Adolescent Psych.

CHUCK. Blow it off.

JEANNIE. Nooo. Hey! Nice place, Earl.

CHUCK. Thanks. Have a seat. I'll get you something to drink.

JEANNIE. I like your artwork.

CHUCK. Cost a fortune. Earl has expensive taste.

JEANNIE. Not in girls.

CHUCK. Here you go.

JEANNIE. *(Laughing.)* Martinis?? Who are you?

CHUCK. Cheers.

> *(He types something.)*

JEANNIE. Why type – it's just easier to just talk.

CHUCK. But that's Earl talking.

> (**JEANNIE** *laughs, and then types. He types something back. It's very suggestive.*)

JEANNIE. Chuck!

CHUCK. Earl. Type it.

> *(She does. He types back. She types back something that surprises him. She is starting to play along. He looks at her. She looks at him, then types again. He's amazed. And*

excited. He types back quickly. Then she does.
They are both getting very aroused. He types.)

JEANNIE. No.

CHUCK. No?

JEANNIE. That's...we shouldn't.

CHUCK. We're not. They are.

> *(She types something. He laughs and types*
> *back. She pauses. Considers this. Types*
> *again.)*

Mmmmm. Wow, babe.

JEANNIE. Type it.

> *(He does. They are rapt on the screen.*
> *Breathing heavily. Typing fast and furious,*
> *over each other. More and more intense.)*

How do I make her move?

CHUCK. Put your, um, mouse...over her.

> *(She does.)*

JEANNIE. How do I move her leg?

CHUCK. Drag your mouse.

> *(She does.)*

Oh my God.

JEANNIE. How do I move her hand?

> *(He gulps.)*

CHUCK. Umm...

> *(She's clearly figured it out.)*

Oh my God.

(They stop typing and just move their characters and watch, transfixed. They each occasionally involuntarily moan.)

(ZANDER bursts on screen. He's holding up a box to show them.)

ZANDER. Hey! Guys!

(They quickly fumble with their controllers in a panic, turning off the game.)

I have had the most fan-fucking-tastic day!

JEANNIE. *(Flustered.)* Yeah? Great! Wow, I should, I should really go...

ZANDER. No! You have to hear this!

JEANNIE. I should be studying...

ZANDER. You don't need to study any more. You're about to be a millionaire.

JEANNIE. What happened?

CHUCK. Rich uncle die?

ZANDER. I went to this seminar today. What is today? Mark this day on the calendar! I went to this seminar that is going to fucking change our lives.

JEANNIE. Wow.

CHUCK. Is this a cult? Do we need to deprogram you?

ZANDER. Joke on funny boy. This is easy, easy money.

CHUCK. Ruh roh.

ZANDER. Where's Ian?

CHUCK. Off peeing in a cup.

ZANDER. Shit. I want him to hear this too. Oh well.

(Going through the box.)

It's called – Proneutra. It's this awesome supplement...
but that's just the...the physical product. What it really
is, it's a way of life.

JEANNIE. I thought you had a job interview.

ZANDER. Baby, this is so much bigger than that. I'm not
going to work for anyone else ever again.

CHUCK. Again? When did you ever...

ZANDER. I'm the head of my own company now. And I
can bring in all of you. I want everybody I care about to
get in on this while it's in its early stages. Because, over
time, all it does is grow.

CHUCK. Like this?

(He makes a pyramid with his hands.)

ZANDER.   Listen. You find other people, other...
entrepreneurs, who want to own something, be part of
something big, like yourselves... And you get them in
on it. And then they get their friends on board...

CHUCK. It's a pyramid scheme.

ZANDER. God Chuck! I knew you would say that. No! It's
NOT.

Or...it is, but so what – it's a fucking awesome product.
It's... *(He grabs a brochure and consults it.)* ...multi-
level marketing. Here. I'm sending you both...

*(He takes a photo of the page, and then texts
it to them.)*

There. Read it. Don't go judging it, bringing all this
negativity, till you read it. And you got to try the stuff.
They gave me one supplement, early in the day. And
look at me.

JEANNIE. Yeah?

ZANDER. Don't I look different to you?

JEANNIE. Maybe...

ZANDER. I feel totally different. I feel powerful, babe. I feel like I could take on the world. And they have supplements for everything. I mean, you gear it to the client's specific needs. Does he want to boost energy, endurance, brain function, metabolism, uh, *(Glancing at the brochure.)* anaerobic threshold – see? It's scientific. It's totally... You have to read the materials.

> *(He's back to rifling through the box he brought in.)*

JEANNIE. So...it's vitamins. Right? Are you selling...?

ZANDER. But it's not. Or it is, but it's way more than that. Once I get some more training – they have these periodic...

> *(IAN comes on screen. He's wearing a button-down shirt and a tie, which he takes off.)*

CHUCK. E-man! How'd it go?

IAN. Hey guys.

> *(He starts playing a war game. We can faintly hear it in the background.)*

CHUCK. Did you get the job? What is the job?

IAN. They're still trying to establish whether I'm a psychopath. And whether my blood and urine are government quality.

JEANNIE. Did they tell you? What the job is?

IAN. They were commendably vague. Chaney vague.

CHUCK. How did they find you? I mean, why you?

IAN. My mad gaming skills and Ninja reflexes.

ZANDER. Dude. Fuck working for the government. I've got this opportunity. For all of us.

CHUCK. Zan's joined a cult.

ZANDER. Shut the fuck up.

> *(He holds up a few bottles of pills.)*

Ian. You have to start taking these. You'll feel fantastic.

IAN. Drug dealer? This is the opportunity?

ZANDER. I'll bring you over some samples.

IAN. So, the first one's free?

CHUCK. *(Laughing.)* Epic fail Z!

ZANDER. Just try them.

IAN. Dude. I'm gonna be peeing in cups for the next year. No thanks.

ZANDER. It's good for you man.

IAN. Is this nine to five drug dealing? What are they paying you?

ZANDER. It's not that kind of job.

IAN. The kind where they pay you?

ZANDER. Stop for a minute and look at the literature.

> *(He texts the brochure to* **IAN** *who continues madly playing.)*

Read it! These supplements are cutting-edge...

IAN. Vitamins are an illusion. They don't do anything. It's proven. They just give you expensive pee.

CHUCK. Man, you are totally obsessed with pee now.

IAN. Where will you peddle your wares? Besides this box?

ZANDER. Well, I only have samples now. But once I get five more people to sell, they'll give me the product.

JEANNIE. You have to get other people to sell in order to sell?

ZANDER. Well, with you three on-board, I only need two more.

JEANNIE. And then we would have to get five more people to sell? Each?

IAN. Boom.

JEANNIE. I don't know babe.

CHUCK. I totally know. I'm out. But, umm...thanks for thinking of me.

IAN. Dude! It's a scam!

ZANDER. You're all so closed minded. This is gonna be one of those things where, ten years from now when I'm on my yacht, sending you postcards from Barbados or wherever, you're going to be like – damn, I could have been in on that but I was a total asshole.

CHUCK. You'd send me a postcard Z?

ZANDER. I'm serious guys. It's your loss.

JEANNIE. So...is that all? You get five people and then you get the product?

ZANDER. Just about. Hey, when's your next class, babe?

JEANNIE. I've got Adolescent Psych at 5. I should really be studying.

ZANDER. Maybe I'll tag along – if we go a little early I can talk to some of the kids. See if I can drum up some interest.

JEANNIE. I don't think Professor Maxwell would / like...

ZANDER. Outside the class. I'm not an idiot. I'll just hang with you outside the class before-hand. Cool?

JEANNIE. I guess.

ZANDER. Dana would be good at selling I think.

JEANNIE. Why Dana?

ZANDER. She looks kind of healthy and athletic. I'd buy vitamins off her.

JEANNIE. Dana?

CHUCK. Oh snap.

JEANNIE. I don't think she's ever worked out a day in her life.

ZANDER. Yeah? She's got that kind of athletic...

JEANNIE. I don't even think she owns sneakers.

ZANDER. Well, whoever you think, babe. You know them better than I do. But I'm pumped! Should we head over?

JEANNIE. It's a little early. I should really study first.

ZANDER. You can hang at the library while I drum up some future...

CHUCK. Entrepreneurs. Like ourselves.

JEANNIE. OK...

ZANDER. Awesome! Love you, babe.

JEANNIE. I'll meet you at the library. Bye guys.

(She's gone.)

ZANDER. So Ian, I need you to do me a solid.

IAN. I'm not pushing your product.

ZANDER. There are some minor start-up fees, just for the / first...

CHUCK. Oh shit! Dude!

ZANDER. Just to get started! I have to give them five hundred.

IAN. You have to pay them to sell their vitamins.

ZANDER. You just have to put money down to – these vitamins are not like what you get at CVS dude. This is some highly developed, scientifically...developed shit. They can't just let you walk out the door with this valuable shit.

IAN. No, dude.

ZANDER. I'm not asking for a handout. I'm just saying, could you hold off cashing that check?

CHUCK. Zan.

ZANDER. Thanks a million E. You'll see that money with interest, within a week. I'm sure of it.

> *(He's gone.* IAN *and* CHUCK *look at each other and shake their heads.)*

CHUCK. Few rounds of *Final Kill*?

IAN. Sure. What the fuck.

> *(The sounds of bombs, machine guns, screams, shouting. They begin maniacally pressing their controllers, transfixed.)*

CHUCK. Is that an / RPG?

IAN. Dude, it's an RPG!! Fire!

CHUCK. Ahhhhhhh!

> *(They disappear as the whole screen is taken up with an explosion.)*

Scene Three

(ZANDER, JEANNIE, and CHUCK all play very intently together, a fantasy MMORPG.)

JEANNIE. OMG. What is that thing?!

CHUCK. Santorg. That club has death rays, so use your shield.

JEANNIE. Yikes.

CHUCK. He's a shape shifter. We've seen him before.

ZANDER. Let's climb the back of that cliff. Come on, babe.

(IAN bursts on, in high spirits.)

IAN. Huzzah! Good day good peoples!

CHUCK. E-man! Grab a controller. We're about to battle a Santorg.

IAN. Why are we up this cliff?

JEANNIE. Wait. What time is it? Oh shit! I missed my Early Childhood Development class. Shit shit shit!

ZANDER. Babe, you're a senior. It doesn't matter anymore.

JEANNIE. It does if I want to go to grad school. Oh shit.

ZANDER. You've got like a 3.9. Relax.

JEANNIE. We've been playing for four hours??

IAN. Stand back guys.

(He brings out the heavy artillery. We hear roaring and then moaning from the Santorg as IAN slays him. JEANNIE and CHUCK cheer.)

CHUCK. Awesome dude.

JEANNIE. That was amazing. What was that thing – like a laser? Where did you get that?

CHUCK. Ian's leveled to 49. He's got all the fun toys.

ZANDER. He really shouldn't be on our quest. It's not right.

CHUCK. Why not?

ZANDER. He should be on his own quest. For his level.

CHUCK. That's bogus.

ZANDER. You should fight at your own level.

IAN. It's cool. I need to clock in on Paraquad. Some dude in New York is paying me a buttload to get him achievements.

JEANNIE. What does that mean?

IAN. I sign in and level him up so he can play his little Wall Street friends and kick their butts.

JEANNIE. You can play for someone else?

ZANDER. It's wrong. It totally taints the games.

CHUCK. Like you don't buy cheats.

ZANDER. I don't man.

CHUCK. Right.

ZANDER. I don't. I wouldn't do that.

CHUCK. OK.

ZANDER. I don't Chuck!

CHUCK. OK dude!

JEANNIE. So, people pay you to play?

IAN. To level them up.

JEANNIE. Really?

IAN. There are warehouses in China with kids playing all day and night to level up these crazy rich guys for like two hundred a week. I can make twice that, easy.

JEANNIE. Wow.

CHUCK. And how was your day at the office dear?

IAN. It was totally outrageously awesome. I passed the wacko test, and now I'm officially employed. They're training me.

ZANDER. Doing what? Just tell us something dude.

IAN. Can't. But I said on the polygraph that I haven't smoked pot in two years, and I passed. So...if someone calls...

CHUCK. Ha! Me too. No pot. No beer.

(He downs his beer.)

JEANNIE. My dad said they're training gamers to do remote missile launches of... *(Trying to remember.)* what is it?

IAN. Why did your dad say that?

JEANNIE. Oh, I told him about how you were interviewing with the NSA and he said that / maybe...

IAN. Why would you tell him that? Shit. Why would you say that? To your dad?

JEANNIE. I'm sorry. I didn't think / that...

CHUCK. Chill dude.

IAN. What exactly did you tell him?

JEANNIE. I just said that you had an interview. I mean, that you were this amazing player. Gamer. And that you had this interview with the NSA. That's all. That's all I know.

IAN. And he said...

JEANNIE. He said maybe they were recruiting you. To do, you know, these remote missile things. Drones! That you were probably operating these drones.

CHUCK. Holy shit. Is that what you're doing, E?

ZANDER. Probably doing some desk job, and he's just acting like he's hot / shit.

IAN. I'm not doing anything yet. I'm just in training. And don't say anything to anyone. I mean it. I signed a stack of papers. That I'm not gonna tell anyone, not even my family.

ZANDER. Yeah, you also said you haven't smoked pot.

IAN. Look. I want this thing. You said I didn't have a real life, right? I should get a life. So now I have a real life, OK? A real job. That I go to every day. So just don't say anything more to anyone.

JEANNIE. I won't. I'm really sorry Ian. / I won't.

ZANDER. She fucking said she wouldn't asshole. You're so self-important about this whole thing. It's so top secret. You signed a fucking / paper.

CHUCK. Wow, Ian. It's so cool. I mean, if that's what you're doing.

IAN. Yeah. It's pretty mind blowing. If that's what I'm doing.

CHUCK. They use you, I mean, these guys they hire, they use them even if they aren't military?

IAN. Well, I'm not the pilot. I'm the S.O. – sensor operator. These awesome pilots who've had years and years in real combat, you know, on the actual field of play, they fly the drones, fire the missiles.

CHUCK. That is so unreal…

IAN. And then the sensor operators use these laser instruments to make sure it goes to its target. And we aim these awesome million dollar cameras that can see fucking everything. So, of course they need people with top-notch skills, you know? Gamers, the top gamers, have awesome reflexes.

JEANNIE. My dad said…oh. Never mind. Sorry.

CHUCK. No, what? We're not talking about you, Ian, we're just talking about these other guys. I mean, if Jeannie's dad knows about it and he's a…

JEANNIE. Dentist.

CHUCK. He's a fucking dentist, then it can't be that top secret. Right?

IAN. How does your dad know all this?

JEANNIE. He read it in the paper. Sorry.

ZANDER. *(Howling.)* HAH!! He read it in the fucking paper! Pwnd *(Poned.)* Ian. It's so top secret! It's in the friggin' news.

IAN. Did I say it was top secret?

ZANDER. What else did your dad read, babe? In the fucking *Reno Gazette Journal*?

(*JEANNIE looks anxiously to* IAN.)

IAN. It's cool. I mean, you can talk about what your dad read. It's got nothing to do with me.

JEANNIE. Well, he said most of the missile, or drone attacks in...

IAN. The Preditor. And the Reaper is the new one.

CHUCK. Wow.

JEANNIE. in Afghanistan and Iraq...

IAN. UAVs. Unmanned Aerial Vehicles.

JEANNIE. They're operated out of here, out of Nevada.

IAN. Creech

CHUCK. Cool.

IAN. Airforce Base.

JEANNIE. And that they use kids, gamers, 'cause there's no way to train people as much as... I mean, no matter how much some pilot could train, he wouldn't have been putting in twenty hours a day for years and years.

IAN. Plus, they're running out of pilots. There are more unmanned vehicles than manned planes. It's insane.

They need more people fast. They'll give me like thirty hours of flight training and then...

CHUCK. Holy shit!

ZANDER. How many guys do they need? Are they looking for more gamers?

CHUCK. *(Laughing.)* Z! You were just ragging on this whole situation. What about your business dude? You're your own boss, remember?

ZANDER. Hey, I totally don't need to work for the government. Clock in clock out. How many hours you work?

IAN. It's gonna be fourteen hour days for a while.

CHUCK. Holy shit.

ZANDER. Fuck that! All I need is two more recruits and I get the product. Maybe Karen, right babe?

JEANNIE. I dunno.

CHUCK. But Ian, this thing is nuts. I mean, you have your hand on the button? What if you fuck up?

IAN. It's not like that. It takes like seventeen steps to fire anything. It would be pretty / hard to...

CHUCK. It's so outrageously cool. You're like a spy.

IAN. Did your dad read about this? For surveillance, they also have these cameras in like, little hand operated planes. Like remote control toys. Your dad read about this, right? I mean, this is general knowledge.

JEANNIE. I guess.

CHUCK. Sure he did.

IAN. And on the screen, it's mind-blowing – it's like you can see everything. It's as good as any shooter game. Better.

CHUCK. You are like, the luckiest dude in America.

ZANDER. What's the big deal? If it's just like the games? He's doing the same thing we're doing, but he has to drive fifty miles to do it.

CHUCK. It's REAL. How long do you train? When do you start bombing shit?

IAN. They don't tell you. You have to be totally perfect for a long time, and then – boom – sometimes you're doing practice missions, sometimes you're doing real ones. You don't know. So it doesn't fuck with your mind when you blow out a village, you know? You might have done it, or it might have just been another simulation.

JEANNIE. But, you're going to really be killing real people.

IAN. Or not.

JEANNIE. But eventually... I mean, it stands to reason that you eventually will. If you keep at it.

IAN. Oh, I'm keeping at it.

JEANNIE. And then... I mean, doesn't that bother you?

IAN. Dude, did you hear what I said? I won't know. I won't know when it's real.

Look, it's not as if *I'm* doing it. I don't give the orders. I don't even know who gives the orders. By the time it gets down to me, it's passed through ten guys. Sometimes I'm just, I mean sometimes the S.O. is just surveilling the area. I'm like, the defense. Sometimes.

JEANNIE. I guess.

IAN. And they're gonna do it. With or without me. But if they use me, it'll be done right. Innocent people won't get killed. Because I'm incredibly skilled. I'll get my target. I won't fuck up. So really, I'm probably saving lives doing it.

JEANNIE. No, you're right. It's good that it's someone who's really amazing and accurate. You're totally right. I just mean I couldn't do it.

ZANDER. Yeah. I couldn't knowingly kill people.

CHUCK. You were just drooling over it dude!

ZANDER. And you know there are always innocent casualties in these things. No matter how accurate you are.

IAN. Well, yeah, sometimes mistakes get made. That's part of war.

ZANDER. Then why do it? If you're killing / innocent...

IAN. So you're saying there should never be any military action. What about fucking World War II? Are you saying we should have stayed out of WWII?

ZANDER. No.

IAN. Ah! So there should be killing, you just shouldn't have to do it. Let somebody else have blood on his hands.

ZANDER. You don't have blood on your hands. You have a little controller in your hands. The blood is like thousands of miles away. You're in some air / conditioned...

CHUCK. Dude. Let's just... It's a totally cool job. I'm jealous as shit. You're going to learn things and see things...we can't even dream of.

IAN. Thanks man.

(He starts playing his game.)

JEANNIE. I can't believe I missed my class. Damn. And I like that class.

ZANDER. So let's go over there. You can get the notes from one of the other kids, right? And I need to talk to Karen. She's so close to signing on.

JEANNIE. I'd hate to run into Casey. She's so awesome. And why did I miss her class? Video games?

ZANDER. You're so fucking sweet babe. They don't notice who's there.

JEANNIE. I dunno.

ZANDER. I'll come by and walk you over.

JEANNIE. I don't know where Karen's going to come up with 500 dollars, Z. I don't think...

ZANDER. Don't worry. They all say they can't find the money, and then they do. Laterz.

CHUCK. Bye Z. Jeannie.

JEANNIE. Bye guys.

(They're gone.)

IAN. You know, if you want to come interview, I could get you in.

CHUCK. Really?

IAN. I mean, no promise they'll sign you on, but they did say if I know anybody with serious skills...

CHUCK. Wow. Thanks, dude.

IAN. No problem.

CHUCK. I really appreciate that.

IAN. I'll give'm your name.

CHUCK. Yeah. But...you know, I don't think so.

IAN. Why not? You meet with them. They give you a bunch of tests.

CHUCK. I've kind of got things good at the casino.

IAN. Dude, how long can you stay there? That's a bad scene. You're gonna burn out man.

CHUCK. Maybe.

IAN. Come on. You're a smart guy.

CHUCK. Nah.

IAN. You need a fucking career. You / can't just...

CHUCK. I don't know. Maybe I'll go back to grad school. In a few years. I don't know.

IAN. Well, think about it.

CHUCK. OK. I appreciate the offer E. I really do. Thanks.

IAN. Sure.

(They each put on headsets and start madly playing in their own private games.)

Scene Four

(IAN is at his screen. JEANNIE comes on.)

JEANNIE. Hey Ian, have you seen Zander?

IAN. *(Jumps.)* Shit! Don't sneak up on me.

JEANNIE. Sorry. Do you know where Zan / is?

IAN. Nope.

JEANNIE. We were supposed to meet at the student union two hours ago. He's not answering my texts.

IAN. How unlike him.

JEANNIE. I'm sure he just got caught up in his recruiting. He's so into it.

I should be studying anyway. Finals are in three weeks.

(Nothing from **IAN.** *He just continues playing.)*

It's totally freaking me out. That this is it, you know?

Did you feel that way? Your last semester?

IAN. No.

JEANNIE. Did you apply to grad school? Oh – duh. Obviously not. I'm glad I didn't and I'm also a little freaked, you know? At least with grad school, you have a few years to put off real life, right?

IAN. Hm.

JEANNIE. But, I figured, No – time to grow up. Spend some time working with actual kids. Rather than just reading about them in a text book.

IAN. That should do it.

(She has no idea what this means. Beat.)

JEANNIE. Whatcha playing?

> (*He presses "share screen."*)

Wow, you're flying! Did the army give you this program?

It's beautiful. You're so good at this.

> (*This makes him blush, which he hates.*)

It's like watching an amazing athlete like...

Oh my God, I've got study-brain. I can't think of any athletes!

> (*He is about to tell her, and then stops himself. Doubles down on his flying. She watches him for a while.*)

Do you mind me watching you?

IAN. No.

JEANNIE. It's not distracting?

IAN. If you stopped talking I'd probably forget you're here.

JEANNIE. Should I stop talking?

> (*He doesn't say anything.*)

You don't like me, do you.

IAN. (*Embarrassed. He does like her.*) I have no real feeling either way.

JEANNIE. Why?

IAN. ...I don't understand what you're asking.

JEANNIE. Is it because I'm Zan's girlfriend and the two of you are best friends and I'm kind of usurping your place, or...taking up the time you would usually spend together?

IAN. You've been studying that psych.

JEANNIE. You think I'm a total idiot, don't you?

IAN. *(Making a joke.)* Well...total...

JEANNIE. *(Done with him.)* OK then. Bye.

IAN. Why are you with him?

JEANNIE. Zander?

IAN. No. Michael Jordan.

JEANNIE. Huh?

IAN. That's the name of a remarkable athlete, by the way. Next time you're trying to come up with a sports simile.

JEANNIE. You want to know why I like Zander?

> *(IAN sighs.)*

I like him 'cause he's smart and funny and...

IAN. Is he smart? Or funny?

JEANNIE. I think he is.

IAN. OK.

JEANNIE. Why do you like him?

IAN. Do I like him?

JEANNIE. You play together – every single day. With him and Chuck.

IAN. Well, Chuck's actually a great guy.

JEANNIE. Yeah.

IAN. And I game with a wide variety of people.

JEANNIE. But those other people are strangers. I mean, you don't really know them.

IAN. But I guess you really know Zan.

> *(Pause.)*

JEANNIE. Zan considers you his best friend.

IAN. Sad.

JEANNIE. Wow.

You want to know why I go out with Zan?

IAN. Nah. It makes total sense. You're attracted to his looks...

JEANNIE. Well, sure, but it's more / than

IAN. And he's attracted to yours. It's very shallow. But, if it works for / you –

JEANNIE. It's more than that.

IAN. No.

JEANNIE. Yes it is. How do you know? Yes it is so. It's his...manner. It's the way he...you know. I like the way he talks. And the way he moves. He has a sort of... charisma. He has this attitude like everything is OK – like it's all gonna work out fine.

IAN. But it might not all work out fine. Given his inability to attend to his most basic human needs...

JEANNIE. He gets by.

IAN. He's a user.

JEANNIE. I think if you have his optimism, that way of approaching the world, things will work out for you. I think that attitude of well-being brings well-being to you.

IAN. *(Pauses the game for a moment to talk to her.)* Our society considers him good looking, and so he's given things. He doesn't have to work for what he gets. And he assumes he'll always be good looking, and he'll always be given an easy ride. That is what you find attractive. That is what draws you to him. That air of privilege. Call it optimism or whatever makes you feel good about your choice, but what you see in him is the cocky arrogance that comes with the easy ride. And you've clearly been on that same ride. So...great. Enjoy the ride together.

JEANNIE. Wow.

IAN. But...what happens if you get acid thrown in your face?

JEANNIE. What?!?

IAN. Or you're disfigured in some other way. Or you get fat. Or you just age badly. What resources will you and Zander have to rely on then? You've blithely gone through life thinking you don't need to develop other strengths.

JEANNIE. I'm in school! I'm studying so that I can actually help someone. Help kids, kids who don't have anyone to turn / to.

IAN. *(Sincere.)* No. You're right.

JEANNIE. That's your fucked-up thing – deciding that's all I'm about. That's you being shallow. That's not me, that's you.

IAN. No. You're right. That wasn't fair.

JEANNIE. Yeah.

(Beat.)

IAN. Chuck was there when you met Zan.

JEANNIE. Yeah?

IAN. And Chuck actually *is* smart and funny.

JEANNIE. No, I know. Totally.

IAN. Both Chuck and I were there. At the Radio Shack that day.

JEANNIE. Yeah. I remember.

(Pause. He goes back to playing.)

But it was Zander who talked to me.

IAN. OK.

JEANNIE. I mean, it was Zander who was joking around. Remember? And then he asked me out.

IAN. Right.

JEANNIE. Any one of you could have asked me out.

IAN. Right.

JEANNIE. But it was Zan who did.

IAN. OK.

> *(Pause.)*

But now it's several months later.

JEANNIE. Yeah?

IAN. And you actually know him.

JEANNIE. Yes.

IAN. And you're still with him.

JEANNIE. Yeah...

> *(They both just sit with that for a moment.)*

Guess I should really go study.

IAN. Yup.

> *(Pause.)*

JEANNIE. You would rather I didn't come on here unless Zan is on?

> *(He says nothing.)*

K. That's cool.

IAN. No.

> *(Beat.)*

JEANNIE. No, it's not cool or...no you wouldn't rather?

(He says nothing.)

Do you mind? If I'm here? When Zan isn't here?

IAN. No.

JEANNIE. Oh. OK.

OK. See you.

IAN. Yup.

JEANNIE. When Zan comes on could you tell him...

(He puts on headphones. Sounds of shooting.)

OK.

(Blackout.)

Scene Five

(CHUCK *and* ZAN *and* JEANNIE.)

ZANDER. After this battle I've really got to go.

JEANNIE. But, I'm coming too, right babe?

ZANDER. You're the sweetest, babe.

CHUCK. I thought I was the sweetest.

JEANNIE. I'm really proud of you.

ZANDER. Thanks. Yeah. After Karen, one more recruit, and I'm golden. I think maybe Amy...

CHUCK. I'm proud of you too, babe.

ZANDER. Then you can be the first to buy some product!

CHUCK. Oh shit.

ZANDER. I'll do a whole workup on you – shoot in some numbers and come up with the exact supplements and nutrients to fit your needs.

CHUCK. I'm aiming for perfectly perfect in every way.

ZANDER. Let's work on some modest goals to start, Chuckstein. Like, let's make you smell less.

> (*They all react to something on the screen. Big celebration!*)

JEANNIE. We did it? Right? We broke through? Is this... Is this it?

CHUCK. Now we must storm the castle!

ZANDER. Laterz. I mean, you guys can keep playing games, but I'm about changing my life and the lives of all I encounter so...

> (*He plays.*)

JEANNIE. But I'm coming with, right?

ZANDER. Nah babe. That's cool. Why don't you just stay here and wait for my triumphant return.

JEANNIE. But I told Karen I'd come by. I think she's expecting...

ZANDER. Back in an hour! Love ya!

JEANNIE. Oh. OK! Bye hon.

> *(He's gone.)*

Love ya.

> *(She sits uncertainly. He's just disappeared on her again.)*

CHUCK. You wanna keep playing?

JEANNIE. I guess, let's wait for Z to storm the castle or whatever.

CHUCK. K.

JEANNIE. Ya.

> *(Awkward.)*

CHUCK. You feel like fixing up Daphne's pad?

JEANNIE. I should really go study.

CHUCK. You can't just leave her homeless. I mean, she's welcome to bunk with Earl, but they might want a change of scenery now and then.

JEANNIE. I dunno, Chuck.

CHUCK. What?

JEANNIE. I think we kinda... I think we crossed a line.

CHUCK. Really?

JEANNIE. I just felt a little weird after. Didn't you?

CHUCK. I felt like I needed some "alone time."

(*They both laugh.*)

It's just play.

JEANNIE. I know.

CHUCK. I mean, they're characters. It's not as if we're really doing anything.

JEANNIE. No, I know.

CHUCK. It was fun, right?

JEANNIE. It was, but I just felt like...

CHUCK. Yeah?

JEANNIE. Like, would we have played the same if Zan had been in the room?

CHUCK. He does role-play too. We should do it with him too some time. I / mean...

JEANNIE. You would have really done, or Earl would have done all that, with Daphne, if Zan had been watching?

CHUCK. I don't know. Maybe not. I don't know.

JEANNIE. Yeah.

CHUCK. Then, let's just fix up your place. Get you some furniture.

JEANNIE. Yeah?

CHUCK. Earl can be Daphne's moving man.

JEANNIE. OK!

(*He fires it up. We hear the music*.*)

---

* A license to produce *Leveling Up (Virtually)* does not include a performance license for any third-party or copyrighted music. Licensees should create an original composition or use music in the public domain. For further information, please see the Music and Third Party Materials Use Note on page iii.

CHUCK. I've given you another 500 credits.

JEANNIE. I can't keep taking your money.

CHUCK. Once Daphne gets a job she can pay Earl back.

JEANNIE. Oh my God. What will Daphne do?

CHUCK. You like this couch?

JEANNIE. No.

CHUCK. OK. Tell me when.

JEANNIE. No. No. Hey! That's like my friend Sandy's couch. In life.

CHUCK. Cool. Where should I put it?

JEANNIE. Put it against that wall.

CHUCK. Yes ma'am.

JEANNIE. Move it down just a little. A little closer to the window.

CHUCK. I like it when you order me around. Why don't you sit and see if it's to your liking. We can exchange it if it's too...

JEANNIE. No. It's great.

CHUCK. Cool. What next? Coffee table... Pictures... Entertainment center...

JEANNIE. Why don't you sit too? See what you think?

CHUCK. OK.

JEANNIE. Good?

CHUCK. Move down a little. I want to see if I can stretch out on it. You know, if Earl and Daphne have a late night playing canasta, and he stays over, he wouldn't want to disturb her in the boudoir.

JEANNIE. Fine fine. Lie down.

It's the perfect length.

CHUCK. That's what she said.

> (JEANNIE *laughs.*)

> (*She types something. He thinks about it. Types something back. Only a few exchanges and they're madly typing again. Moving their characters.*)

> (*They're completely engrossed, breathing heavily and clearly crossing the line* JEANNIE *had been concerned about.*)

> (IAN *comes on.*)

> (*They both freeze. Their characters are in compromising positions.*)

IAN. *(In sullen greeting.)* Peoples.

CHUCK. E! Hey! You just getting in man?

JEANNIE. Hi Ian.

> (*She types to* CHUCK, *but he doesn't see.*)

IAN. Ya.

> (*He begins playing something else.*)

JEANNIE. Chuck. *(Mouthing to* CHUCK.) Off.

CHUCK. Huh?

JEANNIE. Off. Daphne.

CHUCK. Oh! Yeah, sorry.

> (*He moves his character.*)

JEANNIE. I should really go study.

CHUCK. You okay, E?

IAN. Kinda burnt.

CHUCK. Were you flying again?

IAN. Finished my thirty hours. Which sucks. It was awesome.

CHUCK. You're done already?

IAN. I'm doing three months of training in three weeks.

CHUCK. Holy shit.

JEANNIE. You're just coming in...from yesterday?

> (IAN *nods.*)

Morning?

CHUCK. Holy shit dude.

JEANNIE. That's not healthy.

IAN. You think?

JEANNIE. You should sleep.

IAN. It's cool. They're understaffed. Guy who had me up in the plane hadn't slept in like two days. It's just the way it is.

JEANNIE. How scary. My dad said...

> (*They all decide to ignore this.*)

CHUCK. So now you're ready? For real combat?

IAN. I can neither confirm nor deny.

> (*Another awkward pause.*)

CHUCK. We were just outfitting Jeannie's E-Chuck City pad.

IAN. Yeah. I noticed.

CHUCK. Want to join us?

JEANNIE. I should really go study.

IAN. Sure. Why not.

CHUCK. Wow! OK! Cool.

IAN. None of my guys are on anyway.

CHUCK. Great. *(To* **JEANNIE**.*)* Ian is Captain Outstando.

JEANNIE. *(Laughs.)* Awesome. I'm Daphne. Or...she is.

> (**IAN** *brings his character in.*)

Well, hello Captain Outstando. He's cute.

IAN. You go for leotards?

JEANNIE. I like the cape.

CHUCK. I'm gonna show you some tables, lamps, chairs – get the place cozy.

IAN. Here's a couple thousand credits.

JEANNIE. No! Don't! I'll get a job.

IAN. I never play this anymore. You may as well have them.

CHUCK. Awesome. You should get like a grand piano for this room. And a real swag entertainment center.

JEANNIE. Guys. I wouldn't live this way if I won the lottery.

CHUCK. Daphne goes for the nice things in life.

> *(They type a few things to each other.)*

JEANNIE. How do I... I want to offer you lemonade.

CHUCK. Lemonade! Daphne needs a liquor cabinet!

IAN. Walk through here and we'll set up a kitchen.

> *(He starts ordering her things.)*

JEANNIE. I love that! Yellow, OK? Nice. No – I want a breakfast nook!

With bar stools!

IAN. Done. Here's your fridge. Stocked with... *(He clicks the controller.)* lemonade.

JEANNIE. Wow. That's awesome.

OK. You fellas go to the living room and I'll bring you some refreshments.

CHUCK. Yes, ma'am.

(They all move their characters.)

JEANNIE. I'll put yours here. On this very cute end table.

CHUCK. Could you set up a stereo system, E. I want to put on some music.

(IAN does. We hear music.)*

JEANNIE. I love this!

(They all settle in and type and move for a few moments. **JEANNIE** *types.* **IAN** *types.* **CHUCK** *types.* **JEANNIE** *laughs. She types.)*

(IAN types something. Both **CHUCK** *and* **JEANNIE** *look at him.* **CHUCK** *types something back.* **IAN** *types again.* **IAN** *moves his character.)*

CHUCK. What are you doing man?

(JEANNIE is just paralyzed.)

IAN. What?

CHUCK. Don't do that.

IAN. That's not OK? I thought that was OK. That's not OK, Jeannie?

---

* A license to produce *Leveling Up (Virtually)* does not include a performance license for any third-party or copyrighted music. Licensees should create an original composition or use music in the public domain. For further information, please see the Music and Third Party Materials Use Note on page iii.

CHUCK. Cut it out Ian.

IAN. Daphne doesn't like that? It seemed like she does.

> (**JEANNIE** *doesn't know what to say. She sits for another moment and then her screen goes dark.*)

CHUCK. What the fuck?

> (*A beat.* **IAN**'s *screen goes dark.*)

> (**CHUCK** *sits a moment, processing this.*)

Scene Six

(IAN is alone, playing a war game with an online friend. He wears his headset. We can vaguely hear shouting and gunfire and explosions.)

IAN. Look out – there's someone behind that Humvee!

(His friend nails the guy. They enjoy this together.)

Nice!

(We hear chatter over the lines.)

Oh crap. We're going to need more backup... Wasn't Titan 27 gonna meet us here?

I mean – if you say you're gonna show up, show up.

Shit. I don't think we can take 'em alone. Frag out! I'm gonna detonate!

(Explosion.)

Awesome! OK. You lead.

(A beat while they move to another location.)

Hey dude, you ever wonder...what if this thing was real?

But, I mean like...what if those were actual people we were blowing up?

(Something happens on screen. IAN screws up.)

Oh. Shit. Sorry.

Yeah, I'm a little slow tonight. I... I didn't get much sleep.

(Beat.)

But, what if... What if it weren't soldiers you hit.

No, I know. Collateral damage. Totally.

> *(We hear the guy on the other end barking orders faintly.)*

Good one!

> *(He plays.)*

But, listen dude. Say you've got this...this building in your crosshairs, you've been watching it, you know they're keeping weapons in there, you've done your surveillance. You've done your job. You know it's a good target. You get the order, you fire, and just before the missile hits, like two seconds, this kid, this little girl, looks to be your sister's age, this...this little kid walks around the shed out of nowhere. This little...

> *(Something awful happens on the screen. **IAN** covers his face which makes them crash. He is shaken, breathing hard. He comes back in.)*

Oh, fuck man. I'm sorry. I'm really off tonight.

> *(Pause. He is very shaken.)*

Hey, where are you dude?

Hah. No, I mean, I.R.L. I'm in Nevada, are you...

Oh! OK. That's cool. I should really go too, my buddy just got here.

K dude. See you later.

> *(He logs out of the game, and sits alone in the dark room.)*

Scene Seven

(**CHUCK** *is alone, playing. Probably a fantasy game. The sound of a monster on screen.*)

(**ZANDER** *comes on, wild-eyed. For the first time, one of them is outside. He's on the street, video chatting from his phone.*)

ZANDER. Chuck. Have you seen Jeannie?

CHUCK. No. She hasn't been on in like a week. Did she tell you – it got a little weird, last time she was / here...

ZANDER. You got to help me out. I don't know... I don't know what I'm supposed to do here.

CHUCK. What happened? Where are you?

ZANDER. I went to get the product. To the Proneutra /

CHUCK. Yeah?

ZANDER. headquarters...or whatever.

CHUCK. Yeah.

ZANDER. And it's gone.

CHUCK. Do you have the right address?

ZANDER. Yeah, I have the fucking address. The building is fucking here. But... It's empty.

CHUCK. Oh shit.

ZANDER. They cleared out.

CHUCK. Oh, shit man.

ZANDER. I gave them the money. I gave them the money from the five guys I got to sign on.

CHUCK. Fuck.

ZANDER. Jeannie too. I mean, I got Jeannie in on this.

CHUCK. Yeah. Wow.

ZANDER. And...they're gone.

CHUCK. You gotta call the cops man.

ZANDER. Yeah?

CHUCK. You gotta...the better business bureau or...

ZANDER. Do you think there's any way...

CHUCK. What?

ZANDER. Do you think there's any way it could just be... like a mix-up? Like, maybe they moved or... I don't know...

CHUCK. Dude. You were rooked. It was a fantasy dude. It was a con.

ZANDER. Fuck.

CHUCK. Yeah.

ZANDER. Fuck.

CHUCK. I'm sorry dude.

ZANDER. Yeah. Oh fuck. I have to tell all those kids... Jeannie.

CHUCK. Yeah.

ZANDER. Shit man. I should just move. I should just...find a place I can...

CHUCK. Call the cops. You gotta report this.

ZANDER. You think maybe they'll catch them? Get the money back?

CHUCK. No.

ZANDER. Shit.

CHUCK. But, who knows right? Maybe, right?

ZANDER. Fuck.

CHUCK. Yeah.

ZANDER. God Chuck. What do I do?

CHUCK. Well, first you call, before you / even...

ZANDER. No. What do I DO? I mean, what do I do? My life?!

CHUCK. Yeah.

ZANDER. I've got like... I don't know.

CHUCK. You could go for training again – for dealing. You could try craps this time. Or bartending.

ZANDER. I'd have to find a different school.

CHUCK. You would have to show up. Every class this time.

ZANDER. And I'm broke. Totally broke.

CHUCK. Yeah.

ZANDER. I mean, I'm way beyond broke. I owe...

CHUCK. Sorry dude. Really.

ZANDER. I couldn't even swing the cost of the class. Do you think maybe Ian would...

CHUCK. I don't think so.

ZANDER. Yeah. I can't believe it. Those guys were so... I mean it was an awesome product.

CHUCK. Yeah.

ZANDER. It was such a great business. I can't believe this.

CHUCK. Wasn't real man.

ZANDER. Shit. What do I do?

CHUCK. Go to the police station. File a report.

ZANDER. Yeah. Maybe they'll catch them...

If Jeannie comes on, tell her...

You know what, let me tell her, OK?

CHUCK. Good.

   *(**ZAN** just stands, dazed.)*

 (Really worried about him.) You want me to come with you dude?

ZANDER. Would you?

CHUCK. Text me the address. I'll be right there.

   *(He pops off screen. **ZAN** texts him. Pops off too.)*

Scene Eight

(IAN at work. He puts on a headset – different from the one he usually wears to play.)

(We hear voiceovers of the men IAN hears over his headsets, including the pilot who sits to the left of him. The voiceovers are confusing and overlap.)

VO1. Roger received target / fifteen.

VO2. See all those people standing down / there?

VO1. Open the courtyard.

VO3. *(IAN's pilot.)* Pull back. Wide shot.

(IAN does this.)

I estimate there's probably about twenty / of them.

VO4. Hey Bushmaster Element. Copy on / the One-Six.

VO1. That's a weapon.

VO3. Hotel Two-Six. This is Crazyhorse One-Eight. Have individuals with weapons.

IAN. Is that a weapon? Sir? / It looks like...

VO3. Five to six individuals with AK-47s. Request permission to / engage.

IAN. Those aren't... Sir, no confirmation on the / AK-47s.

VO2. Roger that. We have no personnel east of our position. So you are free to engage. / Over.

VO3. Roger. / Go ahead.

IAN. We can't get 'em now because they're behind that building. / Sir.

VO1. He's got an RPG!

IAN. That guy in the front – that may be a camera, / sir.

VO3. All right, we got a guy with an RPG. I'm gonna fire.

VO2. Yeah, and now he's behind the building. God / damn it.

IAN. I didn't... I can't / ID that weapon.

VO2. Just fuckin', once you get on 'em / deploy.

VO3. All / right.

VO2. You're / clear...

IAN. What is he carrying? / That's not...

VO3. All right, preparing to deploy. *(This is to* **IAN.***)* S.O. Prepare to target.

IAN. Yes, sir.

VO1. Let me know when you've / got 'em.

VO3. And... Sensor, on target!

IAN. Roger. On target.

VO3. Currently engaging approximately eight individuals, uh KIA, RPGs, / and AK-47s.

VO2. Hotel... Bushmaster Two-Six. We need to move, time now!

> *(The sound of an enormous explosion.* **IAN** *covers his face as if it's happening in the room.)*

VO1. Yeah, we see two birds and they're on / fire.

VO3. Roger. I got 'em.

> *(***IAN** *is now staring at the screen, heart pounding, out of breath.)*

VO4. Bushmaster Six; this is Bushmaster Two-Six. Got a bunch of bodies layin' / there.

VO2. Yeah, we got one guy crawling around. But, / uh

VO1. We're shooting some / more.

VO2. Roger. You shoot, / I'll talk.

VO1. Hotel Two-Six; you need to move that location once Crazyhorse is done and get pictures over.

VO3. Pull in closer S.O. We need a body count.

> *(But* **IAN** *is frozen.)*

VO2. Hotel Two-Six; Crazyhorse One-Eight. Can we get a confirmation on that body count?

VO3. *(Firmly, to* **IAN.***)* Pull in S.O. Now!

> *(***IAN** *is frozen.)*

Now S.O.!

IAN. *(Snapped out of his stupor.)* Sir!

VO1. Crazyhorse One-Eight; this is Hotel Two-Six / over.

VO3. Oh, yeah. Look at those / dead.

VO1. Nice.

VO2. Good shoot'n.

VO3. Thank you.

VO4. Crazyhorse One-Eight; Bushmaster Seven. / Go ahead.

VO3. Location of bodies.

IAN. *(Checking the map which is over the live feed.)* Mike bravo 5-4-5-8-8-6-1-7.

VO3. Hey good on / the uh...

VO1. Mike bravo 5-4-5-8-8-6-1-7 over.

VO3. This is Crazyhorse One-Eight. That's a good copy. *(To* **IAN.***)* Good work.

IAN. Thank you, sir.

> *(He takes off his headset. There is static on the screen. We hear the sounds of a war game.* **IAN** *looks around stunned, disoriented, out of breath, panting. He's home? There is an explosion on the screen. He jumps.)*

> *(***JEANNIE*** *comes on the screen. She is uncertain when she sees* **IAN**. *Should she leave?)*

JEANNIE. Hey Ian. Have you seen Zan? *(Sees his distress.)* I guess we should talk about...what happened.

Look, it was fucked up, what Chuck and I were doing. It's just a game, but...yeah. So, I don't blame you. For judging me. I'm not gonna do it, play that, any more.

> *(***IAN*** *bends in half and holds his head as if it is aching.)*

Are you OK? Ian?

> *(He doesn't respond.)*

You must be exhausted.

> *(***IAN*** *still has his head in his hands but he grasps his hair in fists as if he is holding himself together.)*

Look, this job – I'm sure you're great at it, of course you are. But it's just not worth it...it's not healthy. And you could do anything. I mean, you're smart and capable and...

> *(He makes a small, anguished moan.)*

I can't imagine what you've seen. So awful. Even if they are, you know, "bad guys," if there are "bad guys" – to have to do that... I mean, they have lives too – mothers and / sisters...

IAN. *(Rocking back and forth, hitting himself in the head.)*
Stoop! Stop! Stop! Stop! Stop! Stop! Stop!

JEANNIE. Ian! Don't!

IAN. IS THIS HAPPENING??

JEANNIE. Ian!

> *(He moves off screen, as we hear him grunting as he pounds himself.)*

(Desperate. Crying.) Oh my God. Ian!

IAN. I can't feel it!

> *(**CHUCK** comes on screen.)*

> *(We get a glimpse of **IAN**'s bloodied face as he thrashes past the camera.)*

JEANNIE. Stop!

> *(**IAN** shouts, an anguished cry.)*

CHUCK. What's going on??

JEANNIE. Chuck, you gotta go over there. Help him!

> *(**IAN** holds his bloodied head and rocks back and forth.)*

CHUCK. What happened? Ian?

Hold tight. I'll be right there.

> *(He pops off screen. **JEANNIE** watches **IAN** rock back and forth, moaning as lights fade.)*

Scene Nine

(IAN, CHUCK, *and* ZANDER *are on.* IAN *is bandaged. Playing, expressionless.* CHUCK *watches* ZAN *pack.*)

ZAN. I think this controller was mine.

CHUCK. No dude.

ZAN. I'm pretty sure I got it when we went to Radio Shack that time to get the cables / for...

CHUCK. Ian bought them.

ZAN. Yeah?

CHUCK. Ian bought the cables too.

ZAN. Wow. I totally thought I bought / the...

IAN. (*Quiet. Expressionless.*) Keep it.

ZAN. Yeah?

(*Nothing from* IAN.)

You sure?

CHUCK. What the fuck, E. He's taking all your shit.

(*Nothing from* IAN.)

(*A beat.*)

ZAN. You okay, man?

(*Nothing from* IAN.)

What happened?

IAN. I don't know.

ZAN. No. But really. Why were you / like...

CHUCK. Leave him alone.

IAN. I don't know. I don't know what happened. I don't know.

(**ZAN** *packs a bunch of things into his backpack.*)

CHUCK. That's Ian's too! God Zander. You don't even have an Xbox. What the hell do you need Ian's shit for? You don't even have a place to live.

ZAN. I'll find a place.

CHUCK. Where?

ZAN. I dunno. I'll just… I'll let you know. I'll be in touch.

(*He jams things into his backpack.*)

CHUCK. Did you tell Jeannie?

Did you? Did you tell her anything? About the vitamins? About you / taking off?

ZAN. I will. I'll tell her once I'm settled.

CHUCK. That is so fucked up Z.

ZAN. I know.

CHUCK. So don't do it. Don't run out. Tell them all you fucked up. Find a way to pay them back. Come on.

ZAN. I will. I'll totally pay everyone back. I will. I just have to find a place, like, make a new start. Get myself situated. I might go back to my parents for just a little bit.

CHUCK. What?? Aw dude!

ZAN. Just till I get my shit together. Come on Chuck. I'm not gonna stay there.

CHUCK. You are. Your mom'll be doing your laundry when you're like, ancient. You'll be thirty-five and like – mom, where's my Scooby-Doo t-shirt?

ZAN. Shut up.

> *(He's filled the bag.)*

OK. Guess that's it.

CHUCK. Asshole.

ZAN. Take care. Both of you.

CHUCK. *(Deep sigh.)* You too, dude. Grow up into a fine young man OK?

ZAN. I'll try.

Bye E.

IAN. *(Still playing his game.)* Bye.

ZAN. I'll be sending you a check soon. Real soon.

IAN. Sounds good.

> *(**ZANDER** closes his laptop.)*

> *(**CHUCK** looks helplessly at **IAN**, still in his own world.)*

Scene Ten

*(A couple of weeks have gone by. **IAN** and **CHUCK** are on screen, each playing his own game. **IAN** plays with little animation. **CHUCK** looks up to check on him now and again.)*

*(**JEANNIE** comes on.)*

JEANNIE. Hey.

(It's like a mirage. He's been dying to see her again, thinking he'll never see her again, thinking she never wants to see him again. And here she is!)

CHUCK. Jeannie!!

JEANNIE. Hey.

CHUCK. Oh wow. Jeannie! Hey! How've you been?

Ian – look! It's Jeannie!

JEANNIE. Hey Ian.

(He looks up and sees her. Nods.)

(Goes back to his game.)

OK! I just wanted to see how you were. Both of you.

CHUCK. Good! We're good!

JEANNIE. Good.

(Awkward beat.)

That's good. OK! Guess I'll be out of your hair.

CHUCK. You're not in...our hair! At all.

(They laugh.)

Hey, you graduated!

JEANNIE. Last week.

CHUCK. All growed up! Welcome to life!

(She laughs.)

JEANNIE. Thanks.

(Beat.)

CHUCK. I guess...you heard from Zan.

JEANNIE. He finally answered after like, fifty calls.

CHUCK. Sorry.

JEANNIE. Yeah.

CHUCK. It was totally fucked up he didn't say goodbye or anything.

JEANNIE. Yeah.

CHUCK. He just freaked about having to break it to everyone. I told him – man up dude. Just do it. But...

JEANNIE. I had to tell everybody. That sucked.

CHUCK. Sorry.

JEANNIE. Karen was here on a scholarship. She has like, no money. Her parents were so pissed.

CHUCK. Yeah.

JEANNIE. Five hundred dollars.

CHUCK. Yeah.

JEANNIE. Guess we were all pretty stupid.

CHUCK. Nah. It seemed like a good thing.

JEANNIE. No, it didn't.

CHUCK. Yeah. No, it didn't.

(They chuckle.)

JEANNIE. I got a job. At a daycare.

CHUCK. Good for you!

JEANNIE. Real life. We'll see how I do.

CHUCK. Right?

(A beat.)

JEANNIE. I guess I should get going.

CHUCK. You can still come hang out. You're really getting good on Hafadai. Level three battle gnome!

JEANNIE. Yeah, I think I'm kind of done with that.

CHUCK. Yeah? OK.

We still need to get Daphne a job.

JEANNIE. I think I'll see how Jeannie does with a job first.

CHUCK. Right.

JEANNIE. You keep Daphne. Get her some nice thigh-high spiky boots and a riding crop.

CHUCK. Done and done.

(A beat.)

Well, we'll always have Facebook.

JEANNIE. Right.

(They laugh a little grimly.)

OK. Good to see you guys. Take care of yourselves.

CHUCK. Hey.

JEANNIE. Yeah?

CHUCK. How would you like to grab a bite?

JEANNIE. You mean...food?

CHUCK. Yeah.

JEANNIE. Real food? Out there? In the real world?

CHUCK. I dunno. It was a thought.

JEANNIE. How will we chat without the little box?

CHUCK. We could text each other at the table.

> *(She hesitates for a moment.)*

Or some other time...

JEANNIE. I could use a burger.

CHUCK. Yeah??

JEANNIE. Yeah.

CHUCK. Awesome!! That's totally...that's just awesome! Yes!

JEANNIE. *(Laughing.)* Cool.

> **(CHUCK** *is about to log out. Looks at* **IAN** *who's still playing.)*

CHUCK. You want to come, E? *(To* **JEANNIE**.*)* Is that OK?

JEANNIE. Come on Ian. You're coming too.

IAN. No thanks.

CHUCK. Dude, you haven't left your room in two weeks. It's time.

> *(A long pause, while they wait for* **IAN***'s response, which doesn't come.)*

JEANNIE. I'll only go if you go, Ian.

CHUCK. Dude!

> **(IAN** *pauses. Going out, being with people is painful, but...he can't let* **CHUCK** *down. He finishes whatever was happening on screen. It takes a few moments. He looks up at them.)*

IAN. Joyner's Grill?

JEANNIE. Yes!

CHUCK. That would be great! Meet you both there!

IAN. Meet you there.

> *(He pops off screen.)*

> *(**JEANNIE** and **CHUCK** look at each other. A small smile. Then **JEANNIE** pops off screen. **CHUCK** alone. A grin. He pops off screen.)*

> *(No one is in the little box.)*

End of Play